ABBE
Regional Library System

HERBERT HENRY

& Santa's Secret Society

Written by
AMBER STEWART

Illustrations by
SÒNIA ALBERT

CURIOSITY BOOKS LOS ANGELES

Herbert Henry & Santa's Secret Society
Based on a story by Russell Hicks and Matt Cubberly
Text and illustrations copyright © 2018 Curiosity Ink Media, LLC
With a tip of the cap to ComicUp!

Library of Congress Control Number 2018950031

ISBN: 978-1-948206-17-4

Printed in the United States of America
October 2018
10 9 8 7 6 5 4 3 2 1

First U.S. Edition

Curiosity Books is a registered trademark of Curiosity Ink Media, LLC

CURIOSITY BOOKS
An Imprint of Curiosity Ink Media, LLC
4352 Forman Avenue, Toluca Lake, CA 91602
www.curiosityinkmedia.com

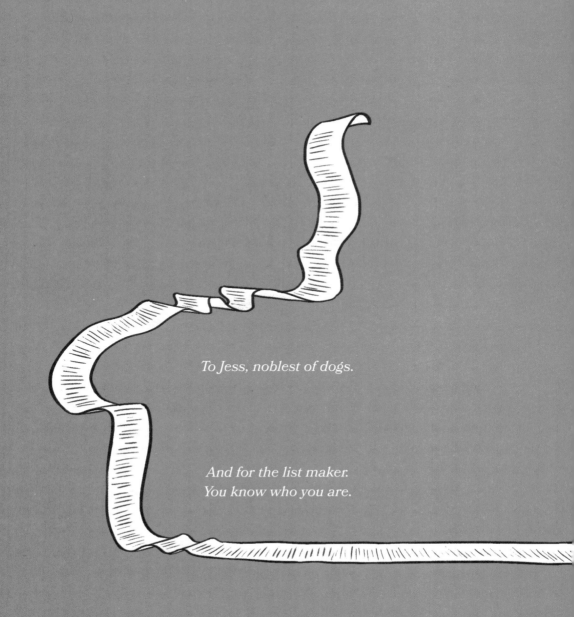

To Jess, noblest of dogs.

And for the list maker.
You know who you are.

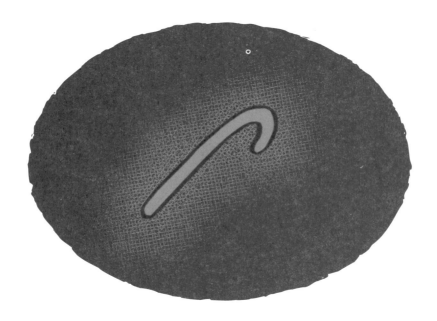

UNLUCKY

DAY
SEVEN

PROLOGUE

Something was wrong. Seven days before Christmas, everyone could feel it. From the Pole up North to the little town of Near North, where our story begins, things were amiss.

Evergreen trees drooped in forests and front windows. Twinkle lights dimmed around doorways. Cakes fell and gingerbread burned in the ovens of the Near North Bake Shop.

That night, a worried young girl stood looking to the North, turning a candy cane round and round in her hand.

Her candy cane glowed a red warning.

DAY SIX

SIX DAYS BEFORE CHRISTMAS

n a snowy morning, in a house so narrow that it seemed jostled by the grander houses beside it, a boy awoke.

"Day six!" Herbert Henry stretched and plucked a list from the dresser next to his bed. Only six days until Christmas morning (five until his birthday)!

Herbert Henry was very nearly ten years old. On Christmas Eve, he would reach double figures, quite the milestone. Mr. Pierre, who owned the Bake Shop in downtown Near North, was already planning a surprise birthday cake with ten candles and many flavors.

For five and three quarters of those almost-ten years, Herbert had been holding on tight to the memories of his mother. Even at a young age, Herbert had made lists of every small and precious thing he remembered about her. He liked the lists. They kept his memories safe.

Slowly, as Herbert and his dad found a new and contented rhythm to their lives, his lists grew more useful and less wistful. Herbert wrote shopping lists, lunch lists, recipes, and homework lists to help run the house and their life. His dad went off to work at the Rosetta Brick Factory to keep their small world on track.

On this day, as our story begins, school was out for the holidays, and Herbert had plans for the day and for all the days leading up to his birthday on Christmas Eve.

But Herbert Henry's tenth birthday would not go as planned.

Herbert stretched again, and nudged the little dog curled beside his bed.

"Time to get up and at 'em, Noble," he said.

"How's it hopping, rabbits?" he said to the carving on his bedpost.

"What's buzzing, bees?" he said to the banister carving.

"Whooo's there?" he called to the owl on the kitchen window frame.

And finally, "Good morning, Dad!" he said to the man who had carved them all.

"Good morning, Herbert!" said Benjamin.

Almost ready for work, he pulled on his coat and tapped his open lunch pail. "What's for lunch today?"

Herbert consulted his Dad's Lunch List. "Cheese and pickle on rye today."

"Lucky me!" Benjamin beamed. "Till tonight, then!" He gave his son a brisk hug and headed out the door.

Herbert and Benjamin were lucky. They had each other, a family of two. Two and a half if you counted the little dog, Noble. Herbert's mom had found Noble shivering on their doorstep when he was a pup. One saucer of warm milk and a bath later, and Noble had never left their cozy home.

Benjamin had built their home for Herbert's mom. He could build anything from wood, with a skill unmatched by any person in Near North and beyond. For every month of

their marriage, he had carved small creatures on bedposts, cabinet doors, stairways, and doorways. They were always slightly hidden, tiny joys to be searched for and marveled over. When Herbert was a toddler, his mother had carried him through their home to discover the carvings. Herbert still greeted them every day.

Sometimes he would rediscover a well-hidden carving, and it would remind Herbert that the only person to match Dad's skill was Santa Claus. Every Christmas Eve, when time ticked across from Herbert's birthday to Christmas Day, a carved creature appeared on Herbert's bed for him to open on Christmas morning.

"How did Santa know I'd like this so much?" Herbert would ask.

"HE JUST KNOWS WHAT MAKES PEOPLE HAPPY,"

his father would answer, smiling.

Long before the house and its carvings, Benjamin had won his wife's heart with a little wooden bird. He had carved it from a precious chunk of wood that was run through with

speckles of color. The bird seemed to glitter in the light as if fluttering its wings to take flight.

The bird was Herbert's now, and he kept it with him always.

Herbert paused as he slipped it into his pocket. Often, he remembered how his mother left a trail of minor destruction through the household, from dropped laundry to floury handprints (and little doggy footprints . . . because wherever Mom went, so did Noble). The floury handprints led to the sweet, homey smell of her baking. Always, Herbert and his father had followed her trail to find buttery cake and kisses.

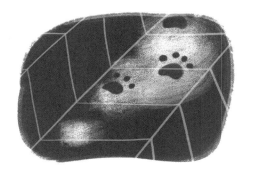

Herbert missed his mother's way of running the house with happy messes. She had always seemed to know just the right amount of this and that to make floors shine, flowers open in jugs, and baths run foamy and warm. Now, just as Dad and Mom had shared the family chores, so did Dad and Herbert. With a list, the chores became fun for Herbert. He was quick to tell his father this when Dad worried that Herbert was growing up too soon.

Today, Herbert had written out his Day Six Christmas list.

DAY SIX CHRISTMAS LIST

☐ TALK TO JACK AT THE TRAIN STATION

☐ BUY DAD'S SPECIAL CHRISTMAS TREATS
    — CANDIED WALNUTS
    — BIG ORANGE

☐ GATHER PINECONES FOR THE PORCH

☐ FIND PINE BRANCHES FOR THE MANTEL

Noble gave a quick bark, as if to say, "Time is ticking!" and pushed Herbert gently with his nose, herding him on to the day.

Herbert tucked away the list and closed the door behind them. Noble paused on the doorstep, sniffing the air. Some undefined scent reached him, drifting on a breeze from the North. Herbert waited, then whistled for Noble to join him. Noble trotted along, watchful for that same something the townspeople felt.

Ahead of Herbert, in the Near North train station, a telegraph clacked out a message. Jack, the stationmaster, and his friend Lily stared at it, listening again and again. It could not be. They had heard of this message, but never thought that they would receive it.

"Save our Christmas?" said Lily, twirling her candy cane. "But . . . that could only mean . . ." She couldn't bring herself to say it. Christmas was in serious trouble.

"We had better ask the others," said Jack. He tapped out a message to all four corners of the world:

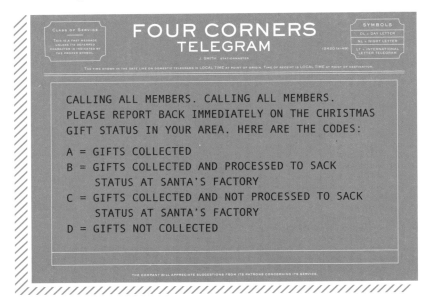

CALLING ALL MEMBERS. CALLING ALL MEMBERS.
PLEASE REPORT BACK IMMEDIATELY ON THE CHRISTMAS
GIFT STATUS IN YOUR AREA. HERE ARE THE CODES:

A = GIFTS COLLECTED
B = GIFTS COLLECTED AND PROCESSED TO SACK
    STATUS AT SANTA'S FACTORY
C = GIFTS COLLECTED AND NOT PROCESSED TO SACK
    STATUS AT SANTA'S FACTORY
D = GIFTS NOT COLLECTED

Slowly at first, then with increasing speed and sound, the telegraph clacked out Cs and a few Ds. The candy cane in Jack's pocket lost its white striping and turned a solid red. Lily pulled hers out of her pocket and stared. "Code Red!" she whispered. "Just like last night! What could be happening up there?"

She and Jack jumped as the station door jangled open.

Herbert smiled at them, bringing unexpected comfort and warmth to the office.

Jack smiled back at him, then saw the thinnest line of white appear on his candy cane. He noticed it on Lily's, too. Jack didn't know quite what that meant, but he had a feeling it was connected to Herbert.

"What is it, Herbert? We're in a bit of jam right now, but is there something quick I can help you with?" Jack stood in front of the telegraph, which was still clacking away.

"I was just wondering . . ." Herbert swallowed. Jack didn't seem his usual helpful self. Herbert felt Noble's cold nose on his hand, nudging him along. "I've been hearing trains at night, Jack, more than usual. Where are they going?"

Jack glanced at Lily and shook his head. "Sorry, Herbert, that's official business."

"But—"

Jack twirled his candy cane in his hand. "Really can't say more."

Herbert stared at the candy cane. "Jack, is that cherry flavored? I've never seen one that's—"

"Okay, time to go, Herbert." Lily's tone was friendly but firm.

Herbert saw that she had the same kind of candy cane. "Do you know where I could get one of those?"

But Lily and Jack were already guiding him out the door.

No answers and no friendship to spare. Herbert trudged away, thinking of Jack and Lily's matching candy canes. Herbert had counted on Jack as a friend. Throughout this winter and last, when the snow hit and school closed, they had played board games that started and paused for weeks. Noble loved being there also. Jack's two lazy cats refused to be corraled, or even moved, from the soft leather chair they lay in all day long. Herding was Noble's favorite game, spinning and nudging and wagging his stumpy tail to his heart's content. Win or lose—and it was always lose with the cats—he was happy.

Lily had appeared early this fall. Jack said she was a friend, and though she seemed young enough to be in school, Herbert never saw her there. He never saw her anywhere but the train station, and never without her hat and her backpack. The backpack intrigued Herbert. It clanked and bulged as if stuffed with an entire supply cabinet. But Lily never opened the backpack and never took off her hat. And though she seemed not much older than Herbert, she never joined in any games. It was as if she was waiting and watching for something, and didn't want to be distracted.

Now it seemed as if Jack felt the same way. They were a team. A team with no need of me, Herbert thought.

He looked toward the mountains beyond his hometown and felt something he couldn't put a name to. Herbert had never known another home. Never known a world beyond Near North. He had never wished for one, so happy was he. Still, something seemed to draw his thoughts North. Shaking off the unfamiliar feeling, Herbert pulled out his list and whistled to Noble, who was busy chasing a family of birds across the field. Herbert had Christmas errands to do, and staring at the mountains wouldn't get them done.

From the office, Jack and Lily watched Herbert leave.

"He saw," Jack said.

"He noticed," Lily corrected him.

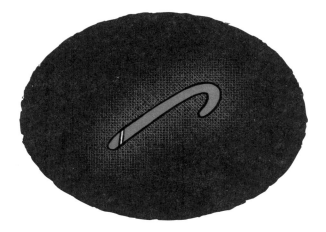

On the other side of town, things were amiss with Benjamin.

Badly amiss.

His workday had begun like any other, in fact, like every other since he could remember. Every morning, Benjamin paused for just a moment, drawing a deep breath before pushing through the huge factory gates. In his lunch pail he carried the sandwich Herbert had made for him. And in his pocket, he carried the little knife that had carved the wooden bird.

"Right," said Benjamin out loud to no one in particular. Pulling back his shoulders, he stepped into his workday at the factory.

As he walked along the factory floor, workers greeted him with hellos, good mornings, and slaps on the back. Benjamin cared about every person who worked in the factory, and they cared for him. He was their foreman, but

a kind boss in their red-brick world. Through the hazy red dust of the factory, Benjamin made sure everything ran smoothly and everyone worked safely.

Day after day, they made hundreds, thousands, millions of endless red blocks all the same size and shape with never a single chip out of place. Any brick with the slightest bump or blemish was chucked on the scrap heap. Useless. No good to anyone.

"No one wants to live in a house with wonky walls," Randolph Rosetta, the factory owner, was fond of saying. He filled the factory with signs that reinforced his brickish philosophy.

Benjamin would think of how much he and his son loved living in their wonky house, and would smile to himself. But he said nothing. He let his carving speak for him. From his first days at the factory, Benjamin had carved his tiny animals into the odd brick here and there. Hidden deep inside deliveries of identical bricks, these secret special stones went out into the world. He didn't know where they landed, but each brick was Benjamin's small gift to a stranger.

At lunchtime that day, just as Benjamin opened his lunch pail, Mr. Rosetta tapped him on the shoulder.

"A word, please, Ben. In my office."

On Mr. Rosetta's desk, Benjamin saw one of his secret bricks: a little cat caught in midpounce on the red stone.

It was one of Benjamin's favorite carvings, although he sensed the cat might now bring him bad luck. Mr. Rosetta cleared his throat, and read the note that had come back with the brick:

Dear Mr. Rosetta,

I am writing to congratulate you on your vision as a brickmaker. I see that you are branching out into making artisan bricks.

We were delighted to receive the cat carving, and once we told our friends, it turns out we are not alone! My cousin has a butterfly carving and my niece has been lucky enough to collect a whole wall of bees over the years. How clever of you to send them as a surprise to your loyal customers. Quite brilliant.

We love our cat so much that we would like to order another 30 of them, please.

Thank you.
Lady Mayoress,
Mid North

"Oh!" said Benjamin, relieved. "That sounds like good news!"

Mr. Rosetta's face grew redder than the brick. Years of sitting behind a desk had not been good for him. He lacked

fresh air and exercise. His childhood had taught him only about the fabled importance of wealth—and bricks—so he also lacked imagination and kindness.

He had not always been quite so cross. As a young

man, he had fallen for the loveliest woman in town. If she had loved him back, things might have been different. But she sensed that he would not make her happy. Nor she him. He was on the point of asking for her hand, when in strolled an artisan who stole her heart away. This artisan, who stood here before him beaming over his defective brick!

"Good news?" Mr. Rosetta shouted. "Do you know how long it would take to make carved bricks? Do you know how much money I—I mean, the factory—could lose on something like this? No, we will not be making special bricks. I'm just going to pretend this got lost in the Christmas card rush."

There were no Christmas cards in his office, Benjamin noticed.

Mr. Rosetta took a deep breath. "This hurts me more than it hurts you, Ben—"

Benjamin doubted that.

"—but rules are rules. We cannot have rogue bricks. We cannot have rogue brickmakers, however good you are. Can't you read the signs? Leave your badge on the way out."

Benjamin took off his badge and turned to go.

"Oh, and Ben?"

"Yes?"

"Merry Christmas."

DAY FIVE

DAY FIVE CHRISTMAS LIST

☐ STIR THE CHRISTMAS PUDDING

☐ CHOOSE A TREE

☐ STRING THE LIGHTS

☐ WRAP THE GIFTS

☐ CHECK OUT THE BAKE SHOP WINDOW

☐ DELIVER THE CHRISTMAS CARDS

Herbert Henry stretched out for his list on the dresser next to his bed. Five days until Christmas (four until his birthday), and he had things to do.

He had heard the trains heading North again last night but he pushed the question from his mind. Christmas was coming, and he had a new list for the day.

"How's it hopping, rabbits?" he said to the carving on his bedpost. "What's buzzing, bees?" he said the to the banister carving. "Whooo's there?" he called to the owl on the kitchen window frame And finally, "Good morning, Dad!"

"Good morning, Herbert," said Benjamin. "What's on the Christmas list today?"

"Wow," said Benjamin, as he quietly stroked Noble's head. "That's quite the list!"

Herbert looked up and noticed for the first time that his father wasn't dressed for work. "Hang on, Dad. Aren't you going to work? Or are you off today?" Herbert felt briefly excited that his dad would help him with today's list.

Benjamin didn't reply. He sat in his chair gently twirling a half-finished carving.

Herbert realized something was amiss. Badly amiss.

"Dad?" he said.

"It's funny. Funny-sad," said Benjamin. "My carving has brought me such joy, then yesterday it turned against me. I lost my job, Herbert. Mr. Rosetta found out about my secret bricks and he didn't like it. Didn't like it one bit."

"But they're great, Dad! He should be happy you make them!"

Benjamin sighed. "He's not a happy man."

Herbert hugged his father. "It will be okay, Dad. More than okay. I know it."

Herbert wasn't as sure as he sounded, so he went back to his list. "The important thing is to get ready for Christmas."

His father nodded. "Why don't you start with that trip to the Bake Shop? They should have today's new scene in the window by now. Take Noble with you. I'll just stay here and finish up this carving." Benjamin picked up his carving knife but stared out the window. Herbert didn't think to look past Christmas. But Benjamin did. And he didn't like what he saw.

Herbert left quietly. What could he do? On any other day, he would have asked Jack. But he was still puzzled by Jack's mood. Maybe his Dad was right. Maybe he just needed some Christmas cheer. The Bake Shop was just the thing for that. Every year, Mr. Pierre counted down the seven days to Christmas with a fresh gingerbread display each day.

Most winter evenings, Herbert and his school friends would press their noses against the Bake Shop window, watching with equal amounts of awe and anticipation as Mr. Pierre put the finishing touches to the display. Noble would run up and down, up and down, keeping the children herded together in a happy group until the baker brought out gingerbread trimmings.

For today, Mr. Pierre had built Santa's sleigh, piled high with cookie-and-marshmallow presents.

As Herbert stood by the window, the Bake Shop door opened.

"Bit of gingerbread, Herbert?" Mr. Pierre held out a basket. "Not my best, though. Having some trouble with the ovens this week."

The gingerbread did taste a bit scorchy, but Herbert ate it anyway. The baker seemed so discouraged.

"The sleigh looks great, Mr. Pierre! Your windows always make everyone so happy!"

Mr. Pierre smiled. "Why, thank you, Herbert. And now you've made me happy."

Just like that, Herbert thought of what his father had told him, year after year: Santa knows what makes people happy.

"Thanks, Mr. Pierre!" Herbert raced back to his house, Noble barking happily at his feet. He went to his room and pulled a sheet from his school notebook.

DEAR SANTA,

MY NAME IS HERBERT HENRY AND I AM NINE YEARS OLD (NOT QUITE TEN YEARS OLD). I KNOW YOU WON'T KNOW WHO I AM AS THERE ARE SO MANY CHILDREN IN THE WORLD, BUT MY BIRTHDAY IS JUST ONE DAY BEFORE CHRISTMAS. I KNOW YOU ARE ALWAYS VERY BUSY ON CHRISTMAS EVE, AND YET YOU FIND TIME TO SEND ME A GIFT. I THINK OF IT AS A BIRTHDAY AND CHRISTMAS GIFT ROLLED INTO ONE. THE ONLY PRESENT I NEED THIS YEAR IS FOR MY DAD TO BE HAPPY. AND YOU KNOW WHAT MAKES PEOPLE HAPPY.

PLEASE MAKE MY CHRISTMAS WISH COME TRUE.

THANK YOU.

HERBERT HENRY

Of course, the letter would work its magic! Herbert dashed to the mailbox but got there just as the mail truck pulled away. Herbert waved, and to his relief it pulled to the curb. The mail carrier jumped down.

"Sorry, Herbert," she said, spotting the address on Herbert's letter. "No more deliveries allowed North this side of Christmas. There's an **SOC** out."

"**SOC**?"

"Yup." She nodded solemnly. "Ask Jack. He'll give you the scoop."

Doubtful, thought Herbert.

The mail carrier added, "I'm heading back to the post office to sort out a family of penguins, special delivery. Someone didn't address them properly, and they got this far before anyone realized they should be heading to the South Pole. Can you imagine!

"The thing is," she lowered her voice, "I seemed to have misplaced one. Hopped out of the truck when my back was turned. Jack and Lily have put a **BOLO** out. So if you spot the little waddler—she is so high and black and white—give them a holler, will you?"

"**BOLO**?" asked Herbert.

"Be On the Look Out," the mail carrier explained.

"Okay. I'll keep a lookout," said Herbert. Inwardly, he sighed. There was that team of Jack and Lily again. And now no way to get his letter to Santa.

The mail carrier paused as she climbed into her truck.

"Herbert," she said, "if your letter is urgent, go to the station now and ask Jack to put it on the train for you. The last train North this side of Christmas leaves at midnight."

She tooted her horn good-bye. "Merry Christmas!" she called as she pulled away.

Herbert stood, so deep in thought that he never noticed the mail truck's back door swing open a bit. A family of penguins jumped down—one, two, three—and waddled briskly toward the train station.

—◆—

That night, Herbert tiptoed into the kitchen and left a note for his father.

Herbert felt he couldn't trust his father's happiness to anyone but himself. He had to hand-deliver the letter to Santa personally. So, feeling quite the adventurer, he quietly closed the door behind him. Herbert knew if Benjamin heard him, he would never let him go.

DEAR DAD,

PLEASE DON'T WORRY, BUT I AM TAKING MY CHRISTMAS LETTER TO SANTA MYSELF. THE ONLY PRESENT I NEED THIS YEAR FOR MY BIRTHDAY AND CHRISTMAS IS FOR YOU TO BE HAPPY AGAIN. AND YOU'VE ALWAYS TOLD ME SANTA KNOWS WHAT MAKES PEOPLE HAPPY.

I AM CATCHING THE LAST TRAIN NORTH AND WILL BE BACK BEFORE YOU KNOW IT. JACK WILL LOOK AFTER ME, I AM SURE.

JUST IN CASE YOU ARE FEELING A LITTLE BETTER WHEN YOU WAKE, I AM ATTACHING MY DAY FIVE LIST HERE! I DIDN'T GET IT ALL DONE.

SEE YOU SOON,

HERBERT

P.S. THERE IS A BOLO* OUT FOR A MISSING PENGUIN (SHE IS SO HIGH AND BLACK AND WHITE). IF YOU SPOT HER, TELL JACK!

P.P.S. *BE ON THE LOOK OUT

P.P.P.S. NOBLE IS COMING WITH ME. HE WOULDN'T TAKE STAY! FOR AN ANSWER.

Even at nearly midnight, in the Near North train station the telegraph still clacked out Cs and Ds. Rumors reached Jack and Lily of idle Elves and unsorted gifts. They resolved to keep the news secret. They could not let the good people of Near North—and all four corners of the world—hear that their children's gifts might not be delivered before Christmas dawn.

They had to save Christmas. Jack would be needed at the station, so it was time to give Lily her chance. She had been waiting for it, she had earned it—and Jack knew Lily was ready to lead the SOC rescue mission.

"Pack essentials only, Lily," instructed Jack.

Lily hoisted her backpack. "Got it all right here, boss!"

"You need to travel light," Jack said.

Lily swayed a bit as she adjusted her backpack. "It's not heavy," she said.

Jack looked at her. Well, everyone has a first mission, he thought. "All right. Go get Christmas back on track. Plan well and make us proud."

"Roger that!" Lily drew herself up as far as the loaded backpack would allow.

Jack smiled, then saw a thin line of white appear on his candy cane and Lily's. "Hold on," he said, "I think young Herbert's about. Look at our canes." The white line grew wider. Another appeared.

From the office, Jack and Lily watched Herbert arrive.

"Do you think we might have been right about him?" Lily said.

Jack nodded. "I think so, maybe."

They both looked back at their candy canes, watching the white lines grow wider.

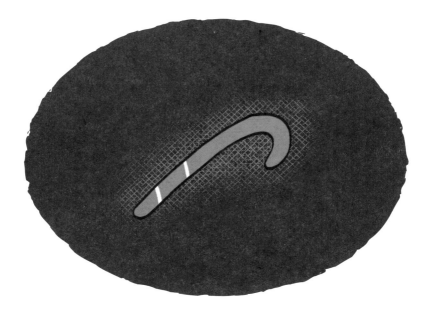

"Don't tell him anything more than you need to, just in case we are wrong," said Jack. "Board the last car so he doesn't see you. Once he's had a chance to settle in, join him in Car 4 for the journey. Keep an eye on him. Keep him safe."

"Roger that," said Lily. "Will you give him that spare candy cane—for emergencies only?"

Jack nodded. "But remember, he doesn't need to know about—"

"Wait!" Lily peered out the window. "Was that the . . . ?"

"The what?" Jack asked.

"No, nothing. I thought I saw the missing penguin. It must have been Noble."

"Must have," agreed Jack, pulling on his stationmaster's coat and heading to the platform. "Wherever Herbert goes, so does Noble."

"All aboard!' Jack called on the platform, candy cane whistle at the ready. "Last train heading to the North Pole tonight! All aboard!"

"Whoa, buddy," Jack said to Herbert and Noble, feigning surprise. "Where do you think you are off to?"

"I'm taking this very important letter to Santa," said Herbert. He hoped Jack would not stop him. Was he still a friend?

"Better take snacks then," smiled Jack, lifting Herbert onto the train and handing him a bag of goodies. "It's a long way and there'll be some stops. Look in Car 4 for a little room. You and Noble should fit right in there. Good luck! Just whistle on this if you need.

he added, popping something into Herbert's top pocket.

Jack blew the all-clear whistle, and the train gathered speed. Herbert and Noble looked out of the window, watching as the platform, station, and Near North disappeared from view. As the train thundered through the night, they settled into their little room. Only then did Herbert remember to check what was in his pocket. It was a candy cane. Just like Lily's and Jack's except this was red and white all over. More white than red, in fact. Was he on their team? Herbert didn't know. Nor did he know the number of stops between Near North and the North Pole or how long he would be away. All he knew was that he was Herbert Henry, not quite ten years old and on a mission to rescue his father's happiness.

DAY FOUR

he lateness of the hour and the movement of the train lulled Herbert to sleep. When he awoke, the train had stopped and the sun was shining.

"Day four!" Herbert Henry stretched. Four days until Christmas (three until his birthday), and he had no idea at all what lay ahead. There was no list to help him today.

"Upper North!" called the Conductor. "Twenty-minute stop! Stretch your legs, grab some breakfast trackside from the Kitchen Cart! Upper North!"

Herbert and Noble joined all the other yawning passengers piling off the train to buy breakfast drinks and buns from a cheery lady with a cart. "You look like a young man in need of hot chocolate," she said.

"I didn't bring any money," said Herbert as the scents of chocolate and cinnamon made his mouth water. The snacks from Jack were good, but not hot and fresh like these.

"Well, then it's lucky I happen to have some free hot chocolate," she smiled, handing him a mug and a plate of breakfast buns.

"I'm Greta. I run the train's Kitchen Car, but at this stop, I set up outside. Always good for everyone to get fresh air."

"Thanks so much, Greta," said Herbert. He was about to say more when a shout interrupted him.

"To the left! TO THE LEFT!"

"What are you talking about? GO RIGHT!"

Herbert watched two short people try to turn around a reindeer and a cart.

"Reindeer, Noble!" Herbert exclaimed. He had never seen any in real life, only heard about them pulling Santa's sleigh. This reindeer's cart was loaded to overflowing with boxes.

"Presents for all the children of the world," said Greta. "Off to the North Pole for sorting. I hope so, anyway. Rumor has it there's some kind of trouble up there. I heard there was even an **SOS** out."

"An **SOC**?" Herbert asked. "What's—"

"STOP! You're making it worse!" the short man holding onto the reindeer shouted.

Herbert looked closer. He was an Elf! So was the other man, pushing uselessly on the back of the cart. There were Elves all around him! Up and down the platform, they loaded the train with gifts and boxes. Herbert had imagined that Elves only lived with Santa, but here they were. And these two needed help. The reindeer at the cart snorted and stamped.

"Excuse me," said Herbert said to the Elves. "You want to turn the reindeer to the right to make the cart go left when going backward."

"Clever," said the Elf at the front.

"Helpful," said the Elf at the back. The cart wheeled into position.

"What do you know, it worked!" The Elves swept off their caps. "Max and Derby thank you."

As Herbert bent to shake their hands, the carved wooden bird fell from his pocket.

"Careful, you've dropped something," said Max. He picked up the bird and stared. "Well, look at that!"

Derby came to look at it.

"There's a story to that bird," said Max, handing it back to Herbert.

"And we have just enough time to tell it," said Derby.

As the Elves on the platform unloaded their cart, Max and Derby waved Herbert over to a worn bench. Max began the tale.

"Long ago, there was young man who made beautiful things from wood. He traveled far and wide, searching through forests to find fallen trees. He carved chairs and bowls and small animals; he liked to think he was giving the trees new life in people's homes. He made his living selling his wares at markets, and was as happy as a person with a wandering spirit can be. One night, he found himself deep in the mountain forest. He was just about to set up his tent when he heard voices quarreling. He pushed aside low branches and brush and to his delight, walked straight onto a tiny village green, surrounded by miniature houses.

"The green was set with a long table and mismatched chairs. Candles flickered in the dusk, and the scene would have been perfect if it hadn't been for the group of small people debating loudly—in other words, arguing—around a large, cold cooking pot.

"Looking more closely, he saw that the villagers were not people, as he knew them. They were Elves. The young man had only ever seen them in his childhood Christmas storybooks, but there they were, large as life—or little as life, as Elves are quite small and sturdy as a general rule."

"Were you the Elves?" asked Herbert.

"No interrupting!" smiled Max. "It'll spoil the surprise."

"We—I mean, the—Elves were arguing about whose turn it was to stock the woodshed and light the fire to heat the pot," Max continued. "Someone had not followed the rota, so the woodshed was empty and there would be no supper . . ."

"I was not next on the rota," argued Derby.

"You were! The rota goes clockwise! Clockwise! You were next!"

"Well, no one told me about the whole clockwise thing," mumbled Derby.

"The rota?" asked Herbert.

"Elf schedule. It's round, and you read it clockwise," said Max, frowning at Derby. "Now where was I? Oh yes!"

"The helpful young man offered to stock the woodshed and light the fire in return for some supper and

a place to pitch his tent for the night. Over the meal he told the Elves that he was a wood-carver. Elves are very skilled—you may or may not know—and it so happened that he had stumbled upon the most talented, most secret of Elf artisans. Yet his skill rivaled even the best of them, such was his talent.

"The Elves asked him to join their secret band of artisans, but he was a wanderer at heart. He visited often over the following months, stocking the woodshed, helping around the village. The Elves looked forward to his visits.

"Then one day, he told them he had fallen in love with a woman in Near North, beautiful and kind. He had nothing but his love and his carving. How could he

dare to ask her to marry him? The Elf Elder gave him a piece of rare forest wood, of a kind and color that he had never seen before. From this single block, the young man carved a small bird that appeared to glitter in the light as if fluttering its wings to take flight."

"And now you have that bird, little man . . . the very same bird."

"The young man became my dad?" wondered Herbert.

"The very same. Our Benjamin. Your dad."

Herbert hardly had time to take it in—he had so many questions—when two things happened at once: he noticed candy canes in the Elves' top pockets, and the Conductor blew his whistle, calling, "All aboard! Last train heading to the North Pole this side of Christmas.

ALL ABOOOOOAAAARD!"

"We've got to go, Noble!" They hopped aboard, but Herbert leaned out the window. "The candy canes!" he shouted. "What do they mean? I have one, too!"

"I can tell you . . ." began Max.

"No, you can't," said Derby. "The train is already moving!"

"Ah, yes, so it is. Quick, take this!" Max pulled a crumpled square of paper from his pocket and tossed it to Herbert. "It tells you the most important uses of the candy cane! Whistle if you need us!" he shouted as the train gathered speed and left Upper North behind.

Herbert wished the Elves could have told him more. What was the secret they seemed to know? Would the note help? He flattened the crumpled paper and read:

CANDY CANE INSTRUCTIONS

1) This is not food. Do not eat.

2) For communication: Whistle once for danger, twice for important news.

3) For indication of danger: Cane will glow red. Note: Cane can also be used for illumination or a flare in such cases.

4) For unexpected obstacles and accidents: Cane can be used to open locks or cans of food and heal small cuts and bruises.

5) Note: Pattern of cane striping may change in positive or negative situations.

Always mind what your cane is telling you!

Odd as it was, the instruction list comforted Herbert.
He took his cane out of his pocket and examined it.
It looked like a regular candy cane, and he was relieved
that he had not eaten it. He was none the wiser why
Jack had entrusted him with a cane. Then he read the
instructions again and remembered Jack saying to him:
"Good luck! Just whistle on this if you need. Once for
danger. Twice for important news."

Herbert sensed that he was still a long way from
knowing the full story behind Jack and Lily, his father's
history, and the Elves he met. For now, though, he
understood that Jack had given him the cane to keep him
safe on his adventure. Jack was still a friend to him.

As he watched, its striping became less red and more
white. Herbert wondered if Greta might know something
more about the candy cane.

He had just stepped
into the Kitchen Car
when Greta burst
out of the walk-in
cooler. "Help! My fish
chowder—it's alive!"

"What!" Herbert saw
then that the stripes on his
candy cane seemed to be dancing,
a little more white than red. What was it telling him?

"In there," Greta whispered.

In the refrigerated little room, Herbert saw a large metal tub of . . . of . . .

"Are those penguins?" he said.

"I don't know! I just took it out and it moved." Greta waved toward the tub.

Herbert tiptoed over to it. Inside, one, two, three, four penguins splashed and slurped the fish chowder. "Dinner and a swim!" Herbert laughed.

Greta began to laugh, too. "You rascals!" she said. "Stop flapping in there! Now what will I do?"

Herbert looked around the Kitchen Car. "It always helps me to start with list," he said. "You must have enough food to make something else."

"I meant about the penguins," she said.

"I'll take care of the penguins," Herbert said, "while you take care of supper."

With Greta's help, he put the tub on a cart and wheeled it out of the Kitchen Car. He didn't know where to take the penguins, but they didn't seem to mind moving as long as they had their chowder. Noble sat on the cart and kept a weather eye on them, nudging each one gently if it looked likely to hop from the tub.

"Are those penguins?"

Herbert turned and saw an Elf peering at the tub. His jacket had bits of hay stuck to it.

"They are," said Herbert. "Do you know where I could put them? They're a bit soupy right now."

"Gosh!" said the Elf. "I've always wanted to go to the South Pole to see them, but now they've come to me!" He looked up, his eyes bright. "I'm Sebastian. In charge of Creatures, Car 3. It's only reindeer at this time of year," he added.

"I'm Herbert. Do you suppose the reindeer would like some company?"

"I know I would!" Sebastian was already wheeling the cart away. "Thanks, Herbert! You made my day! It's been a rough week, what with the **SOC**."

"What's—"

But Sebastian wasn't listening. "Penguins! Lucky me!"

Herbert smiled and pulled out his candy cane. It was nearly white with just a bit of red striping. He didn't have any more answers but he felt that he had made two friends. And really, before he could get any answers, he had to know the questions.

HERBERT'S LIST OF
TRAIN JOURNEY QUESTIONS

— ARE WHITE STRIPES ON A CANDY CANE POSITIVE OR NEGATIVE?

— WILL I MEET MORE ELVES TO HELP ME LEARN THE CANDY CANE SECRET?

— ARE THERE MORE ELVES ON THIS TRAIN?

— WHAT IS AN **SOC**???

—◆—

As Herbert headed North, his father awoke to a quiet house. Herbert and Noble were gone. Benjamin read and reread Herbert's note. He quickly pulled on his coat, heading to the train station, to bring Herbert home.

Even though he knew a bit about the train and the stops it would make, and that Herbert would be safe and well cared for until he could catch up with him, he couldn't help but worry. The station door jangled loudly as Benjamin burst through. Jack looked up from the telegraph machine.

"Jack," said Benjamin, "is Herbert on the train? When is the next one out? Send word and tell him to wait at Upper North so I can go and bring him back."

"Whoa, Benjamin," said Jack. "Herbert caught the last train North. There's an **SOC** out and weather trouble on the tracks, so there's no going after him. He is safe, believe me, he is safe on the train."

"Safe?" sighed Benjamin, running his hands through his hair. "He is only nine!"

"Yes, he is safe." Jack patted his shoulder. "Let him do this for you. He is a young adventurer—just as you once were!—and he is under the care of Lily, Greta and all the train crew. I gave him a spare candy cane. He will use it if there's trouble. He needs you here when he gets back—focus on that."

Benjamin knew Jack was right. As Herbert was with Lily, all would be well. He reread the note once more as he trudged home feeling somewhat more assured that Herbert was quite safe. It hurt him to see that his son thought he needed Santa to restore his father's happiness. Benjamin's happiness lay in one place only—with Herbert. How had he let his son think otherwise?

Benjamin's gaze fell on the Day Five list Herbert had left. Herbert would be back for Christmas, he was sure. It was up to him to make sure that his son came home to the Christmas he deserved. No more sitting about mooning over a lost job. He had never liked it anyway. After Christmas, he would go back to selling his carvings, and perhaps get work building the townspeople's houses. As Herbert had said, it would all be okay—more than okay!

"Right," Benjamin out loud to no one in particular. He straightened his shoulders. "Now what's on this list?" And he . . . - - - -

DAY FIVE CHRISTMAS LIST

- ☒ STIRRED THE CHRISTMAS PUDDING
- ☒ CHOSE A TREE
- ☒ STRUNG THE LIGHTS
- ☒ WRAPPED THE GIFTS
- ☒ CHECKED OUT THE BAKE SHOP WINDOW
- ☒ DELIVERED THE CHRISTMAS CARDS

DAY THREE

ay Three!" Herbert Henry stretched. Three days until Christmas (two until his birthday). He pocketed his list of questions, then set out with Noble to find some answers. His first stop was Car 3.

"Good morning, Sebastian," he called.

"Good morning, reindeer." He patted their strong backs.

"Hello, penguins!" He waved a flappy wave.

"They're happy little fellas," Sebastian said. "Keeping me busy, though."

Sebastian had cleaned out the tub and filled it with water. Now he was feeding the reindeer. Herbert saw that Sebastian didn't have time to talk. He ducked back out into the corridor—and ran right into Lily!

"Good morning, Herbert," said Lily.

"How are you here? Why are you here?" Herbert asked in happy surprise.

"I boarded in Near North, too, Herbert. I'm sorry I didn't come to see you sooner; Jack and I wanted to let you settle in a bit. Shall we sit?"

Maybe she has some answers to my questions, Herbert thought, resisting the urge to pull out his list.

Lily did indeed have an answer to at least one of his questions.

"All around the globe, children wake on Christmas morning and open gifts from Santa Claus. This year—we don't know why—Christmas looks to run late for the first time ever. I am on a very important mission to get it back on track. Jack is counting on me. He instructed me to talk to you now because when you came into the station office the other day, our candy canes began to turn from Code Red to striped again. Somehow you are meant to help Save Our Christmas. Jack and I don't know how yet exactly."

"Save Our Christmas!" said Herbert. "So that's what **SOC** means."

"Yes. I don't know what's wrong, but I'm ready for everything." Lily added.

As Lily showed him the contents of her backpack, Herbert made a list of her supplies.

LILY'S BACKPACK SUPPLIES

WIRE	STRINGS OF TWINKLE LIGHTS
COLD PACKS	SCREWDRIVERS
RIBBON (CURLING AND FLAT)	HAND DRILL
SMALL ELECTRIC FAN	TINSEL
TAPE	WRAPPING PAPER
TWINE	GIFT BOWS
BOX OF SCREWS	

Lily was still unloading when Herbert summoned the courage to tell her his plan.

"But Lily," Herbert took a deep breath, "I am on an important mission of my own. My only reason to catch the train is to give Santa my letter. I must try to rescue my father's happiness."

"Of course," said Lily, "that is important and we will not forget about that. I promise you . . ."

Herbert was unable to ask more as the train shuddered to a stop. Candy canes whistled single blasts. Danger ahead!

"All hands on deck! Snowdrift across the tracks!" called the Conductor. "Grab a shovel. We need to clear it or we'll be late for Christmas!"

Herbert could feel the alarm those words caused. He saw Sebastian and Greta rush past in their coats. He and

Lily jumped down from the train with the other helpers, shovels in hand.

The snowdrift was wider than a grown person and longer than two reindeer and four penguins standing nose to tail. Everyone paused, realizing just how long it would take to clear. The cold cut through their coats as the sun dipped low.

The penguins, for their part, seemed delighted with the drama. Escaping from Car 3, they slid and tumbled without a thought for the Christmas disaster at hand.

"No use standing about," said the Conductor. "Shovels up!"

Everyone raised a shovel.

"Dig!"

And so they did. Even Noble did his part.

But as the shovels touched the center of the snowdrift, it gave a deep groan.

The shovelers froze. No one knew what groaning snow might mean.

Sebastian stepped forward and gently placed his hand on the snowdrift. It sighed.

"It's a snow bear," he whispered. "I think she's injured."

He walked around her twice, looking carefully. Then Sebastian bent over her enormous front paw, braced himself, and swiftly and cleanly pulled out a clump of prickly holly leaves.

"She couldn't walk so well with those, I imagine," Sebastian said. "And the effort must have worn her out. She needs food and water and rest. We have to get her on board."

The large and injured snow bear was not an easy animal to move. It did not help when the penguins tried to slide down her back. But they seemed to get her attention. She heaved herself up and shook them off. Greta got fish from the Kitchen Car and handed it to Sebastian.

Herbert remembered the candy cane instructions about cuts and bruises. Could it help a snow bear? He pointed his cane at her injured paw. The cane glowed red

briefly. The snow bear licked her paw and limped after Sebastian into Car 3, where she gulped down Greta's fish, drank all the penguins' water, and fell fast asleep in the reindeer's sweet straw.

"She'll feel better in the morning," nodded Sebastian.

"Well done!" the Conductor clapped Sebastian on the shoulder.

"Well done, Herbert," said Lily quietly.

"Hot chocolate for everyone!" called Greta.

Over steaming mugs of chocolate, Herbert found himself telling the others about his letter to Santa.

"Be warned, Herbert," said the Conductor. "Santa is very busy at this time of year and now with the **SOC**, he might be even busier. I know he will want to help you in any way he can. He

just may not be able to help you this side of Christmas."

Herbert's heart sank a little at the thought of returning home for Christmas without his Dad's happiness. It must have shown on his face.

"There, now," said Greta, "I'll give you a fresh tray of cookies for him. That will get his attention."

"I'll try to send word ahead," offered the Conductor.

"I'll help you get to him, Herbert," said Lily. "I have made you that promise, **SOC** or not."

"Things will look better in the morning," said Sebastian. This was the advice he gave to animals and friends alike.

Before Herbert fell asleep for his last night on the train, he found himself listing all the friends and adventures he had found on his journey.

His worries faded into a dream of dancing penguins, a snuffling snow bear, and good friends cheering him on with raised mugs of chocolate.

FRIENDS AND ADVENTURES

MAX AND DERBY

GRETA

SEBASTIAN

THE CONDUCTOR

LILY (AND HER BACKPACK)

PLAYFUL PENGUINS

A SNOW BEAR IN THE NORTH

DAY TWO

TWO DAYS BEFORE CHRISTMAS

TWO DAYS BEFORE CHRISTMAS

TWO DAYS BEFORE CHRISTMAS

ay Two!" Herbert Henry stretched and tickled Noble awake. Two days until Christmas (one until his birthday!). Herbert read the list next to his bed and smiled.

Sebastian was right. Everything did look better in the morning.

Just then, someone tapped on Herbert's door.

Herbert opened it and found himself surrounded by four penguins. Noble barked as they flapped on the bed.

"Do you mind watching them, Herbert?" asked Sebastian. "It's getting a bit crowded in Car 3."

"Sure!" Herbert said. "Maybe Santa can get them back to the South Pole."

"Will you ask him?" said Sebastian.

Herbert nodded. "And I'll tell him what great care you've been giving all the animals."

"Thanks, Herbert! Not many people notice what I do." Sebastian hummed a Christmas tune as he hurried back to the snow bear.

Herbert and Noble wrangled the penguins into leashes with ribbon Lily supplied.

"Here are your cookies, Herbert." Greta gave him a loaded tray.

Herbert balanced it on the hand that wasn't holding the penguins.

Lily smiled. "One boy, one dog, four penguins, one tray of cookies and—" she bent closer. "Where's your letter for Santa?"

"In my pocket." Herbert wasn't sure how he was going to get to Santa with the penguins in tow, but he had promised Sebastian.

As the train approached the North Pole, Herbert leaned out the window. They passed a few houses at first, then narrow streets, then wider streets full of merry shop windows. Twinkle lights were strung across the streets between snow-laden rooftops and balconies decked in pine branches. In the main square, someone played a piano under the biggest Christmas tree Herbert had ever seen. Herbert closed his eyes and breathed in the scents of pine and nutmeg. In that instant, he found that he loved this new town as much as he had always loved Near North. Noble must have thought the same, for Herbert felt his tail thumping happily against him.

"Look, Herbert," said Lily. As they passed out of downtown, Herbert saw a circle of buildings in the middle distance. The biggest one stood in the center, surrounded by four others. Each of those buildings was in the shape of a letter: N, E, S, W.

"North, East, South, West!" Herbert exclaimed.

"Sorting Central." Lily looked closer. "And nothing is moving."

Even from the train, Herbert could see the large clear tubes that connected the letter-buildings to the center building. The tubes were stuffed with bright packages.

"This is worse than I thought." Lily gulped.

Herbert patted her arm. "You can do this, Lily."

The train stopped on a jammed platform. From one end to the other, worried Elves stood by reindeer carts piled high with presents. The road to Sorting Central was jammed with more carts. The air hummed with uncertainty.

"We need to find a different way to Sorting Central and the House of Claus," Lily said.

Beyond Sorting Central, Herbert could just make out the lights of a red brick home framed by holly trees and entwined with ivy.

Behind them came a low roar. There stood the snow bear and Sebastian. "Looks as though it's not quite good-bye yet, Herbert," he grinned. "Climb aboard! We'll go cross country."

The snow bear lay down on her tummy, inviting Sebastian, Lily, and Herbert to climb aboard. Herbert unleashed the penguins and let Noble herd them as they dashed this way and that into snowdrifts. He held on tight to the tray of cookies. The snow bear padded away from the traffic, pausing only to growl when they passed holly trees.

Lily and Herbert hopped off at Sorting Central. Noble nudged the penguins inside with them.

In the vast warehouse, boxes and toys lay toppled on the floor. The Sorting Elves stood idle, wringing their hands and looking at the large clock on the wall. The sorting machine had ground to a halt, jammed with presents.

Lily took a deep breath, set down her backpack, and showed her candy cane to the Elf-in-Chief. "Jack sent me to lend a hand. What seems to be the problem?"

"What seems to be the problem?" hollered the Elf-in-Chief. "The List is lost! The List is lost!"

The room buzzed with Elvish alarm.

"The sorting machine levers have been turned this way and that, up and down, on and off. No one knows which present is meant for which sack—North, East, South, or West. We didn't have The List to start

the Seven-Day Sort, so we made our best guesses. The poor machine has overheated, and who can blame it! I feel like overheating myself." She sat down very suddenly, blinking hard.

"*WHERE'S* SANTA?"

asked Herbert.

All chatter stopped. In the silence, the Elf-in-Chief gave a wobbly smile. "Why, Santa . . . Santa's just out for a bit." She looked around. "He'll be back soon," she added loudly.

The Elves murmured in relief.

The Elf-in-Chief took Lily and Herbert aside. "I'm not sure where Santa is. He went off just before the Seven-Day Sort, and no one's seen him or The List since," she whispered.

Lily turned to Herbert. "I'm not sure where to start," she said.

"Start with a list," Herbert said. "Give everyone a job."

Together they made one.

HERBERT AND LILY'S
DAY TWO RESCUE LIST

☐ LILY: FIX THE SORTING MACHINE

☐ ELVES: ORGANIZE THE GIFTS

☐ SEBASTIAN: GO TO THE STATION ON SNOW BEAR AND BRING BACK ANYONE WHO CAN HELP

☐ ASK CONDUCTOR TO DIRECT CART TRAFFIC

☐ PENGUINS: STAND BY FOR DUTY

The mood in the room lifted. The Elves gathered around, and the Elf-in-Chief nodded approvingly at their list. Herbert set down Greta's tray. Cookies could only help at a time like this, he thought, and the Elves seemed to need them even more than he did.

Lily turned to Herbert. "You have the most important task of all," she said. "Find Santa. He must have The List."

Herbert nodded and slipped a few cookies in his pocket. "Come on, Noble." He knew where he would start.

Herbert stopped in his tracks outside the House of Claus. Just above the front door, he saw a tiny bird carved into the brick. A bird that matched the one in his pocket.

He pushed open the door. "Hello?"

Herbert and Noble followed a trail of scrunched-up shopping lists and toy lists into what looked like Santa's study. Herbert picked up a pair of silver spectacles amid half-finished mugs of chocolate in the living room. Then he paused by the flickering warmth of the fireplace.

"Hello, bees?" whispered Herbert. "How'd you buzz up here?" His dad's carving did indeed seem to buzz in the red brick above the fire.

Herbert moved into the hallway, "How's it hopping, rabbits?" he whispered in wonderment, touching the brick carving in the wall.

Herbert followed a buttery smell of baking that reminded him of his mom and home. And in the kitchen, he found Mrs. Claus.

"Why, hello," she said. "Who are you?"

"I'm Herbert Henry, not quite ten. This is Noble. I'm looking for Santa. Everyone's very worried." And I have a letter for him, he added to himself.

"Oh, you must be from the Society." She nodded at his candy cane.

The Society? wondered Herbert.

"Well, I'm worried, too, Herbert. He went up to Lists and Letters and he hasn't come back." Mrs. Claus gestured around the kitchen. Every counter and table was covered with cakes and pies. "I bake when I'm worried."

"Can you tell me where Lists and Letters is, please?" asked Herbert.

Moments later, after he had added his handful of Greta's cookies to a basket of assorted treats, Herbert was on his way.

The door to the Lists and Letters building creaked with the sound of a door that was only opened once a year.

Herbert wandered down aisles of neat wooden boxes, labeled by year. The neatness ended halfway in. Lists and letters spilled from boxes and trailed on the floor. Noble sniffed the floor and ran off. Herbert followed him around a corner.

There, on a small wooden stool, Santa sat peering at a list with a worried frown.

"Hello," said Santa. "And who might you be?"

"I'm Herbert Henry, Sir. Not quite ten years old. This is Noble. My friends and I are here on an **SOC** rescue mission."

"Hmm." said Santa. He noticed the tip of Herbert's letter in his pocket. He had long ago learned to wait for children to tell their Christmas wishes. No need to rush. "Ah! My spectacles! Where did you find them? Thank you, my boy, thank you."

"They were in your living room, Sir," said Herbert. He gently stroked the carving of a leaping cat on the window frame.

"Ah!" smiled Santa. "I see you've spotted my carving. We have them dotted through the house. They arrived in the bricks my lovely wife and I built our home with many years ago. I have no idea how or why, but we have loved them ever since."

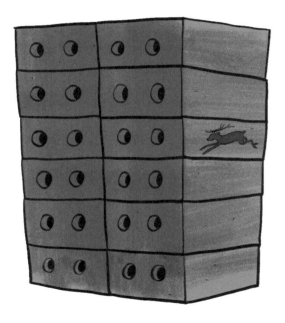

"Mr. Claus, do you have The List for this year?"

Santa tapped his head. "Well, Herbert, it's the oddest thing. Just before the Seven-Day Sort, I went off to a far corner of Sorting Central for a quiet moment among all the hustle and bustle to take one last look at The List. And in that corner, I found an old gift, never delivered. Never delivered, Herbert. It's unheard of. I've been scouring my study and Lists and Letters since to find out why. I have to set it right this Christmas."

"And The List?"

Santa looked uncertain. He put on his spectacles. "I'm sure it will come to me. I can certainly think more clearly with my spectacles on. Now tell me why you are here. It's more than helping me find The List, isn't it?"

Herbert told Santa the whole story: how his very house was made from Rosetta bricks, how his Dad secretly carved some bricks because he was an artist at heart, how Santa had some of these secret bricks, and how his father had lost his job at the Rosetta Brick Factory this very week because of the carvings. How he was Herbert Henry. Not quite ten years old and on a secret mission to rescue his father's happiness. He showed Santa his letter and his little wooden bird.

Santa read the letter and tapped his head again. "That's it, Herbert! Rosetta! I know THAT name! I remember now!" Santa dashed to a wooden box, but instead of pulling out a list, he took out a letter, yellow with age.

Settling back on the stool, he read it to Herbert.

Dear Santa,

My name is Randolph Rosetta. You will know who I am as my family owns the town, the fields, and the mountains beyond. Our family is so rich and so important, I think we might own the North Pole too. I know my parents buy most of my Christmas gifts and most of the time I have no need of you. If you even exist. There is one thing I want: a bedtime storybook that is not about bricks. All my books are about bricks:

101 Things To Do With Bricks (there is only one thing really – building)
Brick Building for Beginners
The History of Bricks
The Brick Prince
The Town Brick and Country Brick

Give me a fairy-tale book, or an adventure book, or a book with heroes and villains and magical creatures. Then I might decide to believe in you.

Or not.

R.R.

"Did you give him the book, Santa?" asked Herbert.

"I couldn't decide, Herbert. He wasn't naughty, but he wasn't very nice either. And he didn't believe in me, not really." Santa sighed. "A child denied an imagination is a sad and terrible thing. I wrapped the book he wished for and set it aside in that far corner of Sorting Central while I tried to decide. Then I must have forgotten about it in the rush of the Seven-Day Sort. And now here we are, all these years later." Santa sighed again. "Seven days before this Christmas, I found his gift and lost The List. Everything went wrong after that."

Herbert nodded. "For us, too."

They sat quietly, each thinking of the unhappiness that had unfolded this week.

Finally, Santa said, "I can give you your wish, Herbert Henry. But I'll need your help first. We need to find that List, or there's no saving Christmas this year."

So Herbert Henry did what he did best.

He made a list.

RETRACE SANTA'S STEPS LIST

- ☐ CHECK THE KITCHEN.
- ☐ SEARCH THE LIVING ROOM NEAR THE SPECTACLES.
- ☐ QUADRUPLE—CHECK THE STUDY.
- ☐ STOP BY THE FAR CORNER OF SORTING CENTRAL.

They worked their way back. (Mrs. Claus stopped baking when she saw them.) There was no List to be found in the kitchen, the living room, the study . . .

Sorting Central was their last hope.

As they passed under the sorting tubes, Santa looked up. "Are those penguins?"

Noble barked, and Herbert saw a blur of black and white flash past in the now-clear tubes.

There was no time to wonder, though. Santa led him to a small back door. And there, in the far corner of Sorting Central, tucked neatly under Randolph Rosetta's long-ago undelivered gift, they found The List!

Santa strode onto the sorting floor. "We have The List!"

The Elves cheered. Lily straightened up and wiped a smudge of grease off her nose.

"Herbert, will you do the honors?" Santa led him over to the sorting machine, which now gleamed, cool and ready to work.

Herbert saw Lily stowing away her cold packs and the fan. Every lever was in place, and every tube was clear. Well, almost.

"One last thing!" The Elf-in-Chief pressed four buttons. The whooshing noise in the tubes stopped, and four penguins dropped back onto the unmoving conveyor belt of the sorting machine.

"They got pulled into the tubes as we were testing them," Lily explained. "But it was a good thing. They gave the present-jam just enough of a nudge to get things moving. After that, they thought it was a game. So we let them play a bit."

Herbert laughed and saw Sebastian rounding up the penguins. Noble rushed in to help. He soon had them lined up and thumped his tail happily. Penguins, it seemed, were better behaved than cats.

Santa looked around at the newcomers and the orderly Sorting Central. "Thank you to all my friends. I will not forget your help." To Lily, he added, "You have done a remarkable job on your first mission." And to Herbert, "You and your new friends make quite the team."

"We couldn't have saved Christmas without you," whispered Lily, squeezing Herbert's hand.

"And I gave Santa my letter," whispered Herbert right back.

The stripes on Herbert's candy cane danced white and red, red and white.

"All right then!" Santa clapped his hands together. "Herbert, would you feed The List into the sorting machine?"

Herbert carefully set The List in the tray. With a whir that sounded as if the machine itself was happy, The List moved forward and gifts began to sort.

As the Sorting Elves cheered and got back to work, Santa leaned down to Herbert. "Rest well tonight. You and I have one last rescue mission tomorrow."

DAY ONE

"Day One!" One day to Christmas Day (and it was his birthday!). Herbert Henry stretched as he woke in the House of Claus. Noble was curled up fast asleep at the foot of the bed. Delicious breakfast smells floated up from the kitchen.

He was Herbert Henry. Today he was ten years old, on his first birthday away from home. What would his father do today without him?

Lily, Sebastian, and the penguins burst into his room. The snow bear couldn't fit through the doorway in Santa's small home but she gave a low growl in greeting. At least Herbert thought it was a greeting. He didn't speak Bear. Herbert reached for his birthday list. Would he find out the answers today?

BIRTHDAY QUESTIONS

WHAT IS THE SOCIETY?

WILL I SEE DAD TODAY?

DOES ANYONE KNOW IT'S MY BIRTHDAY?

"Happy Birthday, Herbert!" laughed Lily, answering that last question. "We are going on a trip. There's just time for your birthday breakfast. Get up, Herbert! Come on, Noble!"

And what a breakfast it was! Mrs. Claus served up cinnamon buns and scrambled eggs while Santa flipped pancakes. And for his double-figure birthday, there were two cakes! Greta came by with jugs of hot chocolate to keep them warm on their journey.

"Herbert Henry," smiled Santa, "you are ten years old today. Double figures! Let's have a look at that birthday list of yours."

Santa read the questions and tapped his head. He did indeed have some answers.

"There's just time for a story before we set off," he began.

His listeners fell into an expectant hush. Even Noble kept still, though watchful.

—◆—

"Lily's Great-Great-Great-Grandma was one of my most trusted workers," Santa began. "She invented, designed, and made the toys that children loved the most. She was also a great planner. In her twilight years she came up with an idea to ensure that those toys would always reach the children who waited for them. A way to support the toymaker Elves and the Elves who do the packing, sorting, and delivery. Each group of Elves is just

as important. And so Santa's Secret Society was born.
Our mission is and always will be to make Christmas
run like clockwork every year.

"All around the globe, children wake on Christmas
morning to open their gifts from me. The Society helps
get them there. Team members organize getting the toys

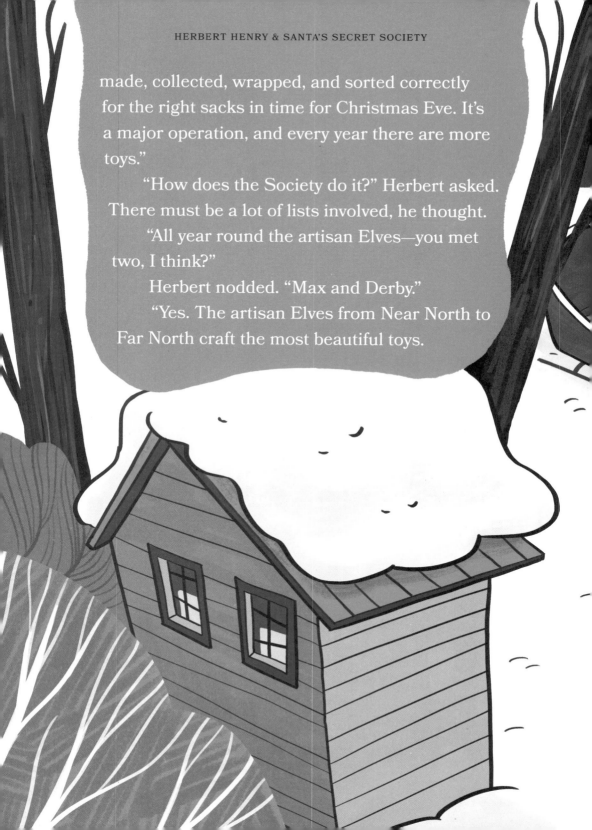

made, collected, wrapped, and sorted correctly for the right sacks in time for Christmas Eve. It's a major operation, and every year there are more toys."

"How does the Society do it?" Herbert asked. There must be a lot of lists involved, he thought.

"All year round the artisan Elves—you met two, I think?"

Herbert nodded. "Max and Derby."

"Yes. The artisan Elves from Near North to Far North craft the most beautiful toys.

From fall onward, each Society member plays a part in collecting gifts from even the most remote Elf villages and hamlets. Elves alone are the toymakers, as it's almost unheard for a person to equal their skill. But anyone with an adventurous spirit and a kind heart might be recruited into the Society. Everyone is given a candy cane as proof of membership. Many Elves carry them, too. The candy cane has many uses."

"I know!" Herbert chimed in, suddenly proud to show off his small piece of knowledge. He pulled Max and Derby's instructions from his top pocket, together with his candy cane. Had he imagined it was striped yesterday? It was almost totally white now.

"But Santa . . ." Herbert took a deep breath. He had so many questions that they tumbled out in a rush. "Why do I have a candy cane? Was it only to keep me safe on the journey? At first, my only mission was to give you my letter. Then Lily asked me to help with the SOC. Will the candy cane help me rescue my father's happiness? How can I join the Society? Is there a test? Should I study to pass? Let me write a . . ."

"Hold on to your reindeer, young Herbert!" laughed Santa. "That's quite the question list. As I say, anyone with an adventurous spirit and a kind heart is able be recruited into the Society. And, as Lily said yesterday, we couldn't have saved Christmas without you.

"You have passed the test many times over. You embarked on an adventure out of love for your father, you helped the Elves with their cart, you used your candy cane to help the snow bear, and you have been a friend to Lily and Greta and Sebastian. You kept the penguins safe—with the help of little Noble here—and you found The List and helped me see the best way forward for Randolph Rosetta and his present. It's an honor to have you, Herbert.

WELCOME *to* **SANTA'S** *Secret* **SOCIETY,** my boy."

Herbert felt that he was glowing as red as a candy cane warning—but for all the best reasons. He, Herbert Henry, just turned ten, was a member of Santa's Secret Society!

"I have telegraphed ahead to let Jack know. Did I mention that Jack is head of Santa's Secret Society?" added Santa.

Jack was head of Santa's Secret Society? The last piece of the jigsaw fitted into place, and Herbert realized that all his questions had been answered. Herbert Henry looked about him and understood that he was now part of a big and happy family—a family of all different shapes and sizes from Greta to Max and Derby to the snow bear. This was his birthday gift from Santa and his friends. He was still Herbert Henry, ten years old, and on a mission to rescue his father's happiness, but now he had a whole Secret Society to help him. Including Jack and Lily.

"There's one thing I don't understand." Herbert turned to Lily. She was still working her way through a stack of pancakes almost higher than her hat. "Santa said your Great-Great-Great-Grandma worked with him. I thought all of his toymakers are Elves."

Lily burst out laughing. "Honestly, Herbert! Have you never noticed my ears?" She pulled off her hat. "I'm half-Elf!"

Herbert blushed, unsure what to say. He was saved by Santa thumping the table, and declaring it was time to get their final rescue mission underway.

And rightly so, Herbert thought. His dad was missing from this picture, and home could only ever truly be where Benjamin was. Soon, Santa, Lily, Herbert, and the four penguins were climbing into

Santa's everyday sleigh. It was slightly built and powered by one huge and feisty reindeer stamping its hooves and ready to fly. Herbert wrapped warm blankets around him and hugged Noble close.

"First stop, the South Pole!" Santa called.

Herbert had kept his promise on the penguins, and had told Santa all about Sebastian.

"So long, fellas!" Sebastian waved to the penguins.

Then with a whoosh that felt like being on a giant roller coaster, they were off.

"Fastest sleigh known to Elf," Santa said.

In a flash, they were easing the sleigh onto the ice of the South Pole. The penguins slid out, circled the sleigh once, then waddled off to join the other penguins. Noble's ears pricked up when he saw the huge colony, but Herbert slipped a ribbon through his collar. "Sorry, Noble. No time for penguin herding today."

Santa looked around with interest. "I've always wanted to visit this Pole," he said. "Right, now Herbert, better warn Jack to expect us. An impromptu Santa visit this early in the day ranks as pretty important, I'd say."

Herbert took out his candy cane and blew twice.

A journey that would have taken days on the train passed in another flash. It was the birthday trip of dreams! Santa landed his sleigh carefully right by Herbert's front door. He pulled a candy-striped lever and winked. The reindeer shook its head and snorted gently, and disappeared. "Secret-sleigh," Santa said. "Don't want people to think Christmas is coming early this year."

Jack and Benjamin, alerted by Herbert's candy cane signal, burst out of the house to meet them.

His father hugged Herbert tight. "I'm so glad to see you! Happy Birthday! But no more missions without telling me," Dad whispered. "Understand? You are my happiness. Not work. Not bricks. You. And Noble, of course," he added as the little dog spun round and round in delight, herding

everyone toward the narrow house's front door.

Benjamin shook Santa's hand, said hello to Lily, and invited them into the house. He put the kettle on the stove and disappeared into the pantry. He came out singing loudly, carrying Mr. Pierre's birthday cake alight with ten candles and spun-sugar sparkles.

"Dad!" exclaimed Herbert in delight, after he had blown out the candles and made a very special wish. "You got ready for Christmas!"

DAY FIVE CHRISTMAS LIST

- ☒ STIRRED THE CHRISTMAS PUDDING
- ☒ CHOSE A TREE
- ☒ STRUNG THE LIGHTS
- ☒ WRAPPED THE GIFTS
- ☒ CHECKED OUT THE BAKE SHOP WINDOW
- ☒ DELIVERED THE CHRISTMAS CARDS

"You left a good list, Herbert." His father tousled his hair.

On the fridge door, Herbert saw his Day Five Christmas list.

"And now it's time to make young Herbert's Christmas wish come true," said Santa. "Benjamin, if you'll come with us . . ."

—◆—

They found Randolph Rosetta in his office. Santa strode in with Jack, Benjamin, Lily, Herbert, and Noble.

Mr. Rosetta jumped up from his desk, turning tomato-red. "Santa," he stammered. "I mean, Mr. Claus. I mean, Sir Claus. I mean, Lord Claus. I mean—"

"Santa will do." He placed a large rectangular gift on Randolph Rosetta's desk. "Now, you should be on the naughty list. Benjamin is just one man bringing up his son all by himself. You fired him because he made a customer happy. It was not a kind thing to do. It was actually a ridiculous thing to do. You need to apologize."

"Sorry, Ben. I mean, Benjamin," said Mr. Rosetta.

"Thank you," said Santa. "Now it is my turn to apologize for your long-overdue gift. I am delivering it now with the hope that it might inspire you to share your happiness with Benjamin."

Mr. Rosetta carefully opened the package. His eyes filled with tears as he stroked the cover of *The Biggest Book of Fairy-tale Adventures Ever Written*. He turned the pages slowly. There were so many stories to read.

Santa cleared his throat.

"Of course, Benjamin! Your old job back! A better job!" his boss exclaimed, holding the book close.

Benjamin surprised them all. "Thank you both. But I don't want my job back."

"But . . . but," stammered Herbert, "I wished for your job back to make you happy."

"My happiness is you, Herbert. A home with you and wood to carve are all I would ever wish for."

Jack stepped in. The stripes on his candy cane spiraled round and round.

"Sir," he said to Santa, "I have received word on the candy cane vine that everything at the House of Claus is in order and ready for you. It's time to get you back for tonight. The secret-sleigh awaits you just outside."

"Indeed, indeed!" said Santa. He stood deep in thought, tapped his head, and turned to Herbert and his dad. "Randolph's loss is my good luck, Benjamin! There's a job for you, if you would like it, helping us all at the House of Claus.

"My Elf-in-Chief and I talked last night about your skill as a craftsman. You are still missed by Derby and Max and

all your Elvish friends from your youth. We would be very pleased and honored to welcome you as a Master Carver at the House of Claus. Think of the toys you could shape! The smiles you could bring every Christmas morning! And you, young Herbert, would be just the one to keep track of The List. I don't ever want to have a year like this again."

Santa smiled at the wonderment on their faces. "I have much to do, and you need time to think. Just send word on the candy cane when you decide."

With a wave and a whoosh, he was off.

Benjamin put his arm around Herbert's shoulders. "Well, Herbert, should we write a list to decide? Two lists, one to stay, one to go?"

Herbert found that he already had a list in mind. "We already belong there, Dad! Your carvings are in the House of Claus, and I just helped with the most important list in the world! Some of the Elves already know you, and I've made such friends! They are like family! You'll get to see the snow bear and . . ."

Herbert continued his list as they headed home for their last—and very best—Christmas in Near North.

CHRISTMAS DAY

CHRISTMAS DAY

CHRISTMAS DAY

CHRISTMAS DAY

CHRISTMAS DAY

DECEMBER TWENTY-FIFTH

verything was right. Everyone could feel it. From the Pole up North to the little town of Near North, Christmas Day dawned just as it should.

Evergreen trees stood straight and tall in forests and front windows.

Twinkle lights glowed around doorways.

Cakes rose and gingerbread baked in the ovens from town to village.

And in a house so narrow that it seemed jostled by the grander houses beside it, Herbert Henry awoke.

"Christmas Day!" Today he was ten years old and one day. He had a job in Santa's Secret Society. He had a father who beamed with happiness. And he had a present on his bed to open. Carefully, he unwrapped it. A little wooden bird lay in his palm, carved from a precious chunk of wood that was run through with speckles of color. The bird seemed to glitter in the morning light as if fluttering its wings to take flight. It was the perfect match to the other bird. They would be together always.

Herbert Henry touched the bird gently, stretched, and plucked a list from the dresser next to his bed. The list was simple but joyful.

CHRISTMAS LIST

☐ WAKE DAD WITH A HUG AND A BIG
MUG OF CHOCOLATE

☐ GIVE DAD HIS SPECIAL CHRISTMAS TREATS:
– CANDIED WALNUTS
– BIG ORANGE

☐ USE THE CANDY CANE VINE TO CONTACT
NEW FRIENDS IN SANTA'S SECRET SOCIETY

☐ WISH ALL A MERRY CHRISTMAS!

LUCKY

DAY SEVEN

$SEVEN$-DAY $SORT$
One Year Later

ay Seven!" Herbert Henry stretched and plucked a list from the dresser next to his bed. Only seven days until Christmas morning (six until his birthday)!

Herbert Henry was very nearly eleven years old.

Since his last birthday, Herbert has kept his two wooden birds on his dresser. He always says good morning and good night to them. And there they stay throughout the day, keeping his memories safe.

Since moving to the North Pole, Herbert's lists have grown and changed as much as his family and friends. Herbert still writes shopping lists, lunch lists, recipes, and homework lists. But he is also now keeper of The List for

Santa; chief note-taker for Jack and Santa's Secret Society; and recorder of all the new toys his father designs and carves for children to open on Christmas morning.

On this day, as our story ends, school in the North Pole was out for the holidays, and Herbert had plans for the day. Today started the Seven-Day Sort.

Herbert carefully put The List into the tray. With a whir that sounded as if the machine itself was happy, The List moved forward and gifts began to sort. Beside him, Lily, Benjamin, and Santa smiled. Noble thumped his tail.

The Elf-in-Chief blew a sigh of relief. A calm and orderly Christmas was under way.

With his work done for the day, Herbert thought back to all that had happened since last year. There was so much, he decided to make a list.

The fairy-tale book did indeed help Randolph Rosetta become a kinder person. He still reads a chapter every night before bed and no longer dreams of bricks. Soon after Santa's visit, he realized the town was full of artisans almost as skilled as Benjamin. Now, the factory makes carved bricks, wonky bricks, wooden bricks and things that are not bricks at all. The town flourishes with craftspeople coming from far and wide to work there.

GRETA DECIDED TO STAY AT THE NORTH POLE. SHE OPENED A BAKE SHOP IN TOWN. SHE LOVES TO VISIT HERBERT AND BENJAMIN'S COZY HOME IN A NARROW HOUSE ON A SNOWY STREET. SHE OFTEN TEACHES HERBERT NEW RECIPES WHEN SCHOOL IS OVER. SOON, HERBERT THINKS AND HOPES, SHE AND BENJAMIN MIGHT NEED TO START A WEDDING GUEST LIST.

SEBASTIAN HAS BECOME A PART OF SANTA'S SECRET SOCIETY AND IS NOW ASSISTANT REINDEER KEEPER FOR THE CHRISTMAS SLEIGH TEAM. SOMEDAY, HERBERT HAS A FEELING, HE WILL BE IN CHARGE OF THE CHRISTMAS SLEIGH TEAM. FROM TIME TO TIME THEY SEE THE SNOW BEAR IN THE MOUNTAINS. SHE STILL AVOIDS HOLLY.

LILY'S SAVE OUR CHRISTMAS RESCUE MADE HER A LEGEND IN SANTA'S SECRET SOCIETY. SHE STILL KEEPS HER BACKPACK FULL AND AT THE READY, BUT DIVIDES HER TIME BETWEEN NEAR NORTH AND THE NORTH POLE. SHE PROMISES TO ALWAYS BE ON HAND FOR THE SEVEN-DAY SORT. SHE AND JACK AND HERBERT WILL ALWAYS BE A TEAM.

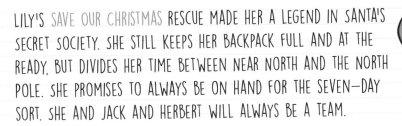

JACK CONTINUES AS HEAD OF SANTA'S SECRET SOCIETY AND KEEPS THE TRAINS RUNNING ON TIME. HE HAS MOVED INTO HERBERT AND BENJAMIN'S OLD HOUSE AND IS STILL DISCOVERING THE CARVINGS THROUGHOUT. AND AFTER MEETING THE LADY MAYORESS'S NIECE IN THE BAKE SHOP, HE NOW HOPES TO FILL THE NARROW HOUSE WITH LOVE AND CHILDREN.

With Benjamin's help before the big move North, Randolph fulfilled the Lady Mayoress's request for cat bricks. Sometime after he delivered them, he asked for Benjamin's help again—to build a wooden house (with just a few carved bricks) for his new wife and him.

Noble has found plenty of people and creatures to gather up in his home at the North Pole. Every day is a new adventure for him.

And Herbert?

There is just one more thing to say.

Herbert Henry has kept his promise to never again go on a Santa's Secret Society mission without telling Dad first.

The End

ABOUT THE AUTHOR

Amber Stewart is a British writer who spent her early childhood in London before moving with her family to rural Dorset, in the furthest reaches of southwest England, where she spent much of her time staring out of the window waiting for something to happen.

She graduated from University College London with a degree in Russian Literature and began an ongoing and acclaimed career in children's book publishing, both as an author and editor. Her award-winning picture books, in partnership with the artist Layn Marlow, depict the everyday happy triumphs and challenges of childhood. Amber has two grown up children and lives once more in London.

—◆—

PRAISE FOR AMBER STEWART

Too Small for My Big Bed
A beautifully illustrated (the spread-eagled, sleeping Piper will melt your heart) and touchingly sweet story about growing up and taking the first steps towards independence. - Daily Mail

Little By Little
Sometimes you pick up a book and you just know that you're going to love it—and this is one of those books. The illustrations are a delight with muted colors capturing the spring countryside and the animals to perfection. The text is a delight to read aloud. It's simple and direct but it expresses exactly how Scramble feels. The book is highly recommended. - Bookbag

'Liquid, lithe and Lyrical..'
Carousel on Bramble the Brave

—◆—

ACKNOWLEDGEMENTS

Huge thanks straight off to my publisher for trusting in my storytelling ability and making me believe that I could write several thousand words just as well as I could a few hundred for my picture books. I would have stumbled for sure if it had not been for the ideas, discussions and freedom he and the team at Curiosity Ink Media afforded me. Also to Catherine, the best editor across the pond any author could have. I am as ever so grateful to my agent Nancy Miles who–aside from being a brilliant agent and good friend–always makes me laugh.

Even though he would have had absolutely no idea who I am, I would like to acknowledge the 1950s artisan furniture maker Robert Thompson, the 'mouseman' of North Yorkshire. As a kid, I was shown the signature mice he would carve into the pieces he crafted–so the chair, table, bowl or whatever it was became uniquely his and also a unique joy for a child to discover. I carried this memory with me all through my life, hoping at some point to weave it into a story–and now I have! I hope he would be pleased; it is certainly an homage to his work and to my own childhood. It goes without saying, but I will say it anyway, that I am forever in my late parents' debt for giving my siblings and me a childhood full of words and pictures.

—◆—

ABOUT THE ILLUSTRATOR

Sònia Albert is a Spanish illustrator currently living in
Cambridge, England. She was born in Barcelona and was
raised in Mataró, just a step off the mesmerizing
Mediterranean Sea.

After graduating from Pompeu Fabra University in Barcelona
with a degree in Audiovisual Communication, she studied
illustration at La Llotja art school. Soon after graduating,
she started working in comics illustration at ComicUp studio,
and is now working on a master's degree in Children's Book
Illustration at the Cambridge School of Art. Sònia is eagerly
looking forward to filling children's books with
her creations . . . her true passion.

—◆—